The Happy Hippopotami

By **Bill Martin Jr**   Illustrated by **Betsy Everitt**

Harcourt Brace & Company

San Diego   New York   London

Library of Congress Cataloging-in-Publication Data
Martin, Bill, 1916–
The happy hippopotami/by Bill Martin Jr; illustrated by Betsy Everitt.
p.   cm.
Summary: The happy hippopotami enjoy a merry holiday at the beach, wearing
pretty beach pajamas, dancing the maypole, and battling with water guns.
ISBN 0-15-233380-8
ISBN 0-15-233382-7 pb
[1. Hippopotamus—Fiction. 2. Beaches—Fiction. 3. Stories in
rhyme.] I. Everitt, Betsy, ill. II. Title.
PZ8.3.M4113Hap   1991
[E]—dc20   90-37921

G F E D C B

Printed in Singapore

The paintings in this book were done in gouache on Bristol kid finish paper.
The text type was set in Palatino by Thompson Type, San Diego, California.
Color separations by Bright Arts, Ltd., Singapore
Printed and bound by Tien Wah Press, Singapore
Production supervision by Warren Wallerstein and Michele Green
Designed by Camilla Filancia

For Roger and Judy Bredahl
—B. M.

For Chris
—B. E.

BEACH →

Happy hippopotamuses
  Climb aboard the picnic buses
For a hippoholiday
  In the merry month of May.

Happy hippopotami
  On the sunny beach do lie
Like a stretch of granite boulders
  Except, of course, for sunburned shoulders.

Happy hippopotamamas
Wearing pretty beach pajamas
Spread tons of cheese on soda crackers
To feed the hungry crackersnackers.

Happy hippopotapoppas
    Stroll about the candy shoppas
Giving children dimes and nickels
    To buy their favorite poppasicles.

Happy hippopotadaughters
Dive into the shallow waters
Splashing waves in stormy motion
Rocking ships across the ocean.

Happy hippopotasons
Fill their trusty water guns
And gallop out to squirt the foe
Like a cowboy picture show.

Happy hippopotapooses
 Toddling boldly on the looses
Stuff the pockets of their britches
 With gooey jelly sandywiches.

Happy hippopotamisses
Dance the maypole, throwing kisses
To a crowd of gentlemen
Who throw the kisses back again.

Happy hippopotamisters
    With hippy hair and hippy whiskers
Rock and roll their steel guitars
    Hoping they'll be TV stars.

Happy hippopotapilots
  Glide about in eagle flylets
Rising on the sudden breezes
  Whenever any hippo sneezes.

Happy hippopotamights
  Dressed in polka-dotted tights
Vie for hippopotaprizes
  Lifting weights ten times their sizes.

Happy hippopotamezes
  Fly about on high trapezes
Somersaulting through the air
From way up here . . .

    to way down there.

Happy hippopotapreachers
  Call the hippos to the bleachers
For a ton of appreciation
  And another ton of inspiration.

At last the happypotamuses
Climb back aboard the picnic buses
With a "Hippo-ray! Hip-hippo cheer!
Until we meet again next year!"